P9-DXK-752

Tuck's Haunted House

Story and Pictures by

Martha Weston

Clarion Books ◯ New York

For Dinah, who is not easily scared.

Thanks a bazillion.

Clarion Books
a Houghton Mifflin Company imprint
215 Park Avenue South, New York, NY 10003
Copyright © 2002 by Martha Weston

The illustrations were executed in watercolor and pencil.
The text was set in 15-point New Aster.

www.houghtonmifflinbooks.com

Printed in Singapore.

Library of Congress Cataloging-in-Publication Data

Weston, Martha.
Tuck's haunted house / story and pictures by Martha Weston.
p.   cm.
Summary: Tuck, a little pig, doesn't want his younger sister, Bunny, to mess up the haunted house
he's building in their garage, but he doesn't realize that her help could lead to a really good scare.
ISBN 0-618-15966-5
[1. Haunted houses—Fiction. 2. Halloween—Fiction. 3. Brothers and sisters—Fiction. 4. Pigs—Fiction.] I. Title.

PZ7.W52645 Tv 2002   [E]—dc21   2001055268

TWP   10 9 8 7 6 5 4 3 2 1

It was Halloween.

Tuck was making his first-ever Haunted House.

It was in the garage.

It was going to be perfect.

Tuck planned to scare the bejeebers out of all his friends.

"BOO!" said his little sister, Bunny.
"I'll help! I know how to be scary."

4

"You don't scare me," said Tuck. "Besides, you're too little. You'll just mess things up."

5

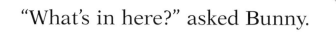

"What's in here?" asked Bunny.

Monster's

"That's the Monster's Coffin," said Tuck. "Don't touch it."
"There's no monster in it," said Bunny.
"Leave it alone," said Tuck. "It's perfect the way it is."

Bunny went into Tuck's Tunnel of Doom.

"This needs to be crookeder," she said.

"You're wrecking it!" said Tuck. "Get out of there!"

But Bunny was already smushing her doll into the Cauldron of Worms and stirring up the noodles.

"Stop it!" said Tuck.

"But it's nice and gross now," said Bunny.

"Bunny, stop messing up my Haunted House!" said Tuck.

"It's not just *your* garage," said Bunny. "I can be here if I want."

"Well, it's my Haunted House," said Tuck.

Bunny started to cry.

"Oh, here," said Tuck. "You can add a little toilet paper to the Mummy."

Tuck started peeling grapes
for Ghouls' Eyeballs.

Bunny got pretty carried away with the toilet paper.
"Hey! That's too much!" said Tuck. "Take it off."

But Bunny was dancing around,
squealing a Halloween song.

"QUIET!" shouted Tuck. "Sit down here
and don't make a sound, or I'm telling Mom."

Bunny sat.

Tuck finished peeling the grapes. He hung up the rest of the wet string for the Icky Drippy Forest. He fixed the Tunnel of Doom.

Tuck looked around. His Haunted House was ready.
And it was perfect.

Tuck got his costume on just in time.

"Come in . . ." he said, in his spookiest voice. He flipped off the lights.

It was really dark.

"What's that?" a cowboy whispered. "I hear something."

Tuck heard it, too. It was creepy.

"It's . . . um . . . a ghost snoring," he said.

But what *was* it?

Tuck quickly dropped to his knees and led everyone into the Tunnel of Doom. It was even darker inside. It seemed to go on forever.

"Eeeww!" a clown said. "I crawled on something squishy."

"Ghouls' Eyeballs," said Tuck. "Try one. They're delicious."

"You first," said the clown.

Tuck picked up a grape. It felt slimy, just like a real eyeball. "It's only a grape," he told himself and put it in his mouth. It started to slither down his throat. "Gaah!" said Tuck.

"Eeeww!" said everyone else.

As he was trying to swallow, Tuck heard the noise again.

Tuck took a deep breath. "Beware of the Ancient Mummy," he said. "And here is the Cauldron of Worms."

"What's *in* there?" asked the princess.

"An Evil Monster Baby," said Tuck.

Everybody squealed and backed into the Icky Drippy Forest.

But Tuck was listening for the noise.

Suddenly, Tuck heard a moan behind him. He whirled around.
Something was rising up from the Monster's Coffin.
Something awful! Something with no face!
The creature was staggering toward him.
"Tuuuuuuck!" it wailed.

Tuck screamed and ran. He could hear the thumping feet of the monster right behind him.

He could feel its hot breath on his neck.

Crash! Down went the Cauldron of Worms. Out flew the noodles and the Evil Monster Baby.

Tuck slipped and skidded out the door.

Shrieking cowboys, a princess, a clown, and a carrot thundered past him.

Out came the wailing monster, tripping and falling onto Tuck.

"EEEEEEKKKKK!" squealed Tuck.

"Tuck!" cried the monster. "I was calling you! Why did you run?"
"Bunny?" gasped Tuck.

"I woke up and it was all dark!" said Bunny. "Oh, Tuck, I was so scared!"

"I . . . bet . . . you . . . were," panted Tuck.

"Why did everyone run away?" asked Bunny.

"Because of the monster," said Tuck.

"A *monster?* Where?" squealed Bunny.

"Right here," said Tuck, giving his sister a squeeze.

"Me?" said Bunny. "Wow!"

Then she smiled. "I told you I can be scary."

Bunny leaned against Tuck.

"But *you* weren't scared, were you?" she said.

"Of course not," said Tuck.